My Holiday Love
Friends to Lovers Series
by
Reba Bale

Table of Contents

---

1.   https://paperorpixels.com/

About This Book

Her new roommate is down on her luck...and easy on the eyes.

When Ashley's roommate moves out unexpectedly, she needs to find a new one fast. There's no way she can afford Seattle rent by herself on a receptionist's salary, so when her friend recommends the new barista at their local coffee shop, Ashley jumps at the opportunity.

Hannah is new in town. She's looking for a fresh start after getting fired, dumped, and evicted all in one week. By a stroke of luck, she lands a job and an apartment in one visit to the funky little coffee shop she visits to use the free Wi-Fi.

She and Ashley could not be more different, but they seem to click anyway. When the friends and roommates realize neither of them has anywhere to go for the holidays, they decide to make their own Christmas right in the comfort of their apartment. When a little too much eggnog leads to a passionate kiss in front of the Christmas tree, suddenly these friends are seeing each other in a brand new light.

Can they move past their differences to find forever? Or will their relationship be as temporary as the holiday season?

"My Holiday Love" is part of the "Friends to Lovers" romantic novella series. Each book in the series is a steamy standalone featuring an LGBTQ couple making the leap from friends to lovers and looking for their "happily ever after".

Be sure to check out a free preview of "The Divorcee's First Time" at the end of this book!

Dedication

This book is dedicated to everyone who learned the hard way that sometimes the family you make is far superior to the family you're born with. Be sure you spend your holidays with the people who really matter.

Join My Newsletter

Want a free book? Join my newsletter and receive a copy of my book "Hotel Spanking" for free. You can expect to receive an email two to four times a month with new releases, bonus chapters or special sales. Go to bit.ly/rebabooks to sign up today.

Hannah

"Can I get you a refill?"

I looked up from my computer at the tall, slim woman standing by me with a coffee pot. She was cute in a girl-next-door kind of way, with her hair up in a messy bun and the freckles across her nose. A little younger than me, not that I should be looking. Not after everything that had happened. Besides, she was wearing an engagement ring.

"Um. How much is it?"

The young woman's nose crinkled. It was adorable. "You get free refills of drip coffee while you're in the café."

I sighed in relief. I was dead broke, and another cup of coffee would help me forestall having to eat for a while. I needed to make my meager savings stretch as far as possible. Plus, drinking another cup of coffee would give me an excuse to keep using the Wi-Fi.

"Okay then, yes please, I would love another cup of coffee."

The woman filled up my cup and looked me over curiously. "I'm Camille by the way."

"Hi Camille, I'm Hannah."

"Are you new in town? I'm pretty good at remembering faces and I don't remember seeing you here at Morning Jolt before."

"Yeah, I'm new to Seattle," I answered, immediately put at ease by Camille's friendliness.

Her eyes went to my computer screen where I was scanning the job listings. "Are you looking for a job?"

"Yeah."

"Well, not to be too pushy or anything, but one of our baristas just quit if you're interested in food service work. My manager Bob was just about to post it online. I can send him out here to talk to you about it if you're interested."

My eyes widened. "Really? That would be great."

"No problem." She slid her phone out of her pocket and tapped it a few times. "I just texted him to stop by when he's free. Have you worked at a coffee shop before?"

"Yeah, it's been a few years though."

"Well, coffee's not changed much," she laughed. "It's hard work and you have to be here at ungodly early hours, but this is a great environment and Bob is a good manager. Firm but fair."

Thirty minutes and a coffee demo later Bob had offered me a job. It seemed almost too good to be true.

"Can you start tomorrow?" Bob asked. "No problem if you can't come on such short notice, but we're down a barista and could really use the help."

"Tomorrow works perfectly," I responded quickly. "What time?"

"We open at five thirty on weekdays. I'll need you here to set up and start brewing coffee at five o'clock. Camille here will show you the ropes."

"I'll be here," I promised.

I didn't care how early I had to start, I was just grateful to find a new job so soon. I'd been in town less than a week. As Bob hustled off I turned to Camille.

"I can't thank you enough."

She waved her hand dismissively. "You were just in the right place at the right time, and fortunately for you, you know your way around an espresso machine."

I grabbed my laptop bag that I'd stored behind the counter during the demo. "Okay, well thank you all the same. I'll see you in the morning."

I got to Morning Jolt ten minutes before my shift, ready to start my new job. For the first time in a while, I was feeling hopeful about my future.

My life had been going along pretty well until recently. I had a decent job working at a tattoo parlor and I was living with a woman who, while things weren't perfect with us, I figured we'd get married eventually.

Until the day I came home to find the apartment empty. And I mean empty. Other than my clothes and personal effects that were dumped on the floor, everything was gone. Every stick of furniture, every morsel of food, every towel and blanket, every dish, even the toilet paper. Gone.

I'd texted my girlfriend Mona in a panic, thinking maybe we'd been robbed, and she'd responded, "I'm done. I can't do this anymore. Sorry." Then she'd blocked my number. I still didn't know what had happened or why she'd robbed me, it wasn't like we had anything nice anyway. Worse yet, it was the last day of the month, and I didn't have enough money to cover her share of the rent.

I'd gone to my boss to ask for an advance, leading to an uncomfortable conversation where he told me that they'd just declared bankruptcy the day before and were closing the shop. They'd been planning to tell the employees that same day. At least I'd gotten my final paycheck.

In the space of twenty-four hours, I'd lost my girlfriend, my job, and nearly all my Earthly possessions. And without money for rent, I was homeless too. I'd driven out of Portland in a panic, not stopping until I hit Seattle three hours later. I couldn't say what drew me here, other than some unexplained instinct, but maybe it was fate that I'd wandered into this coffee shop.

Now that I had a job, I just needed to find a place to live. Who could have guessed Camille would have the solution to that too?

"What part of town do you live in?" my new coworker asked me during a break.

"Uh." My mind raced as I tried to remember the name of a Seattle neighborhood. Any Seattle neighborhood.

My panic must have shown on my face because Camille stepped in front of me and gave me a stern look. "Hannah. What's going on?"

"I'm kind of between houses right now?"

She frowned at my questioning tone.

"What do you mean?" she asked. "Where did you sleep last night?"

"In my car."

She sighed deeply, as if my answer aggrieved her. She looked around to confirm we were alone and then said, "Spit it out, sister. What's going on?"

I gave her the highlights, or the lowlights really, of my last week, trying hard to be emotionless. Saying it all out loud made me want to cry, something I hadn't allowed myself to do. I'd learned long ago that crying didn't help anything. When I was finished with my story, Camille gave me a probing look.

"If someone ran a background check on you, would the information match what you just told me?"

"Yes!" I said, offended. "I'm broke and pathetic, but I'm not a liar."

"Well in that case, I think I have a solution to your housing problem."

Ashley

My phone buzzed just as I walked out of my apartment. It was my friend Camille. We'd met at a local author's conference and clicked immediately. We both self-published fantasy books and we'd become each other's feedback partners. It worked well for both of us, and in between critiquing each other's storylines we'd become good friends.

Camille: *Are you coming to Morning Jolt?*

Ashley: *OMW, why?*

Camille: *I think I found you a new roommate.*

Well, this was good news. My steps lightened as I headed towards the coffee shop a few blocks away from my apartment. Although my books were starting to get some traction, I wasn't anywhere near making a full-time living with my writing. Unfortunately, that meant I had to spend my days working as a receptionist at a real estate company, which was quite possibly the most boring job in the world.

I'd been sharing an apartment with my best friend Brian for years, but he'd recently moved in with his girlfriend. He'd very kindly prepaid me three months' rent as a notice, but the longer I looked for a decent roommate, the more nervous I was getting. I'd interviewed one loser after another. I hoped whoever Camille found wasn't a psycho. I was starting to get desperate. Seattle's housing market was expensive, and I was paying a premium to be in a nice, safe neighborhood close to work. I didn't want to have to move.

I pushed open the door to Morning Jolt, my eyes going to my friend. I waved to her as I went to the back of the line. Morning Jolt was always busy at this time of the day. At least they'd finally found someone to fill that open barista position. I checked out the newbie while I stood in line.

She was about my age – maybe early to mid-thirties – and average height, with pale white skin, large brown eyes, a pert nose, and a chin that was the tiniest bit pointy. Beneath her Morning Jolt apron, I could see curvy hips, a trim waist, and generous breasts. With her blue hair and tattoo-covered arms she looked like the stereotypical Seattle grunge girl.

"Oh hey Ash, good timing," Camille greeted me when I reached the counter. "There's a break in the line behind you."

She pointed to grunge girl. "Ashley, this is Hannah, our new barista. Hannah, my good friend Ashley."

"Nice to meet you, Ashley," Hannah said politely.

"You as well."

"Hannah just moved to Seattle, and she's looking for an apartment. Since you're looking for a roommate, I thought you two should meet." Camille stepped away from the counter. "I'll let you two chat while I make Ashley's coffee."

"Where did you move from?" I asked.

"Portland."

When Hannah didn't elaborate I went into a description of the apartment. "I have a two bedroom apartment about four blocks from here, in a secure building. There's a large kitchen, dining room, living room, a washer dryer in the unit, a bathroom with a clawfoot tub, and a large balcony. It's also got hardwood floors and built in cabinets and shelves throughout the unit."

Hannah looked impressed. "Wow, that sounds incredible. How much is the rent?"

Her eyes widened slightly as I told her the rent and average utility costs. "Um..."

Just then Camille returned with my nonfat caramel macchiato. "You can afford it, Hannah, unless you have a lot of credit card bills or something?"

Before Hannah could respond Camille added, "You haven't seen the tips yet, trust me you'll clear anywhere from fifty to a hundred bucks a day on tips as long as you stay on the morning shift."

Hannah looked relieved. "In that case, when can I come see it?"

We made arrangements for her to come that same evening after I got off work. For some reason, I was looking forward to seeing her again all day. On the surface, we seemed very different, so I wasn't sure what that was about. Maybe I was just relieved that I might have a new roommate soon. After living with Brian for so many years I really missed having someone else in the apartment.

Hannah met me promptly at six o'clock, following me around as I showed her the features of the apartment. When we got to the open bedroom I said, "I'll get this air mattress and dresser out of here before you move in. I had a friend from college come to visit and she used the air mattress. My last roommate left the dresser behind, and I've been using it for storage."

"You don't have to do that," she said quickly. "I mean, if you don't need them."

"Won't you want to bring in your own furniture?" I asked.

Hannah's face flushed. "I don't have any furniture."

"None at all?"

She shook her head. "My um, my last girlfriend, um, took it when she left."

"Wait, your girlfriend robbed you?" I asked, ignoring the little thrill of receiving confirmation that she was a lesbian too. "Feel free to not answer this if I'm being too nosy, but what happened?"

Hannah met my gaze. "I have no idea. I thought everything was going fine with us and then I came home one day, and everything was gone from our apartment. And I mean everything. Her stuff. My stuff. Other than some clothes of mine, she left me with nothing. Thank God I had my laptop, phone, and car with me, otherwise that shit would probably have been gone too."

"Jesus Christ, that's rough. I'm sorry. Did you report it to the cops?"

"Portland cops don't come for something like a robbery," she explained. "They're so short-staffed you have to be in the middle of murder to get a response, and that's only if you're lucky."

"Is that why you moved here?" I asked. "Because of your break-up?"

"Kind of. The day after I discovered that she'd stolen all my shit I went to work and found out the tattoo shop where I worked was closing. The rent was due the next day and I couldn't afford it on my own, so I gave the key to the landlord, packed my handful of clothes in a trash bag, and drove here on a whim. Then Camille adopted me, and here we are."

This had to be one of the craziest stories I'd heard but for some reason, I believed Hannah. Maybe I was being naïve, but her expression seemed to be a mixture of mortification and pain and I really didn't think she could fake that.

"Wow. Okay. Well, I'm willing to try this out if you are?" When she nodded I said, "Let's go see the building manager about getting you an application to be a sublessee."

Hannah

Camille and Ashley were either the nicest people on Earth, or the craziest. Without knowing a damn thing about me, Camille had convinced her boss to hire me, contingent on my background check coming back clear. It would, but neither she nor the boss knew that. Then she'd convinced Ashley to sublet this fan-freaking-tastic room to me.

This apartment was easily the nicest place I'd ever lived. And after hearing about how my ex, or She-Who-Shall-Not-Be-Named, robbed me blind, she'd just trusted that I was telling the truth. I could have been making the whole thing up. I could be a serial killer. I had the strangest urge to take Ashley over my knee and spank her for being so trusting. Not that I would. I really wanted this apartment.

I studied her as the building manager input my application into the computer and ran my credit and background checks. She looked about as opposite from me as she could be. Where I was curvy, she was slim, although we were about the same height. My hair was blue and edgy, where hers was a honey blonde with artful highlights, cut in an uber professional bob.

Everything about her was perfect, from her symmetrical features, to her straight white teeth, to her subtle make-up. She looked like she'd be at home in the Hamptons, or one of those places where rich people hung out.

Her pale white skin appeared completely unmarked by any ink, although you never knew these days. She could totally have a little butterfly or a rose on her thigh, something tasteful that she got on a spring break trip or something.

She looked up, catching me staring at her, and her golden brown eyes widened.

"What? Do I have something on my face?"

I had to laugh. Ashley was so freaking vanilla. I bet she dated guys named Rob or Keith. But I didn't care about any of that. One thing that was clear, Ashley was a kind and generous soul, and in my book that beat everything else. Obviously, she wasn't homophobic either. She hadn't even batted an eye when I'd talked about having a girlfriend earlier.

"No, sorry, I was just spacing out."

"Okay Hannah," the building manager said, "Your credit and background check look good, I just need you to sign the building rules and the sub-leasing agreement with Ashley and you'll be all set. Please read everything carefully."

Twenty minutes later I was officially a resident of the Union Arms Apartment. It felt good.

"We should go out and celebrate," Ashley said, reading my mind. "Do you want to grab dinner? I mean, if you're not busy?"

"Sure, that would be nice."

Now that I knew I had a job and a place to stay, I could use a little of my meager savings from my final paycheck to have a celebratory dinner.

"There's a great local brewpub up the street if you're a beer person. They have burgers, salads, macaroni and cheese, that kind of thing."

"Sure, that sounds great."

I was surprised. I thought Hannah would be more of a wine bar girl but looks could be deceiving I guess. Or maybe they had appletinis and crudites at this brewpub, it was Seattle after all.

"Great, let me just change out of these clothes and we can go."

We headed upstairs and Ashley gave me a key to the apartment before going to change. She came out a few minutes later looking like a completely different person. In place of her expensive work clothes, she was wearing faded jeans that were ripped at the knees, a tight tank top with an unzipped Huskies hoodie over it, and a battered pair of Nikes. Her face was scrubbed of make-up and her shoulder-length hair was pulled back into a messy ponytail. She looked adorable.

"Wow, that's quite the transformation."

"I know, right?" Ashley laughed, and it was the sweetest sound I'd ever heard. "I have to dress for success at my job, but if I had my druthers I'd never wear anything but jeans and yoga pants."

We headed out in the opposite direction from the coffee shop to a bustling restaurant that took up an entire block. Ashley led the way, finding us a booth in the corner, and sliding me a menu from the rack on the table.

"Everything's good here, but I'm partial to the burgers."

The waiter came and we both ordered a burger and a beer. It was funny how appearances could be deceiving. An hour ago, I would never have imagined that Ashley would step foot in a place like this, let alone order a beer while wearing ripped jeans and a hoodie.

"Tell me about this job you have to dress fancy for."

She rolled her eyes. "I'm the receptionist at this commercial real estate company. The money and benefits are good, but it's boring as shit. I use like five brain cells to do my job, but it's a good way to support myself while I work on my writing."

"Your writing?"

"Didn't Camille tell you?"

I shook my head. "Tell me what?"

"I'm a fantasy writer. That's how we met, at a writer's event."

"Hold up. You're a writer? A fantasy writer? And so is Camille? I had no idea!"

"Yeah." She picked up her phone and clicked a few times before sliding it over to me. "That's my website. I sell my books on all the major retail platforms."

I scrolled through the pictures of book covers featuring busty women fighting dragons and other mythical creatures. "Holy crap, you've published ten books?"

"So far."

"Wow, that's impressive. Truly. I'm totally going to read one of your books."

"Don't tell me if you do, in case you hate it."

I laughed.

"Why do you need a roommate and a job? I guess I thought all writers were millionaires."

"Most writers make less than a thousand dollars a year, actually."

"Wow, that's depressing. Well, what's your plan with your writing?"

"I'm trying to increase my earnings every year and have each book be more profitable than the last. And I'm putting all of my profits into a special bank account so that when I get enough saved I can buy a house."

"Isn't it all profit?" I asked.

"No, when you self-publish you have to pay out of pocket for things like your book cover, proof reading, advertising, that kind of thing."

"Why not publish with a company then?"

"I like the flexibility of publishing myself, keeping a higher percentage of my profits, and keeping creative control."

"That makes sense."

Ashley and I continued chatting as we ate our burgers and fries. I was surprised how much we seemed to have in common despite our superficial differences. We had many similar interests.

I'd spent most of the last ten years immersed in the lesbian community in Portland and hanging out with the same people. Maybe it would be good for me to live with a straight girl for a while so I could broaden my horizons. I'd had a bad habit of going from relationship to relationship without a break. I needed to avoid distractions. Hanging out with Ashley might be just what I needed to help me focus on myself while getting my life back together.

Ashley

"How's it going living with Hannah?"

Camille and I were meeting for a monthly writing sprint session at her house, but in between our sprints we took a break, talking and catching up.

"It's going great. She's a little guarded and quirky, but I like her. She's quiet, cleans up after herself, and she never steals my food. Win, win."

"I knew you two would get along," Camille said. "Any sparks though?"

"What? We're roommates."

"You're also both single."

"I don't think I'm her type," I said. "I haven't got any attraction vibes from her at all."

"But you are attracted to her?" As usual, Camille jumped on what I wasn't saying as much as what I was.

"I mean sure, she's hot. But she's also a great roommate and starting to be a good friend. There's no way I want to ruin that. The last thing I want to do is have to find another damn roommate."

"Well, if you're not going to go for Hannah, maybe you should try that dating app that matched me up with Madison. It seems to have a really high success rate. Let's face it my friend, you've been in a long dry spell."

"Maybe I will."

***

Three weeks later...

"Are you sure your friends won't mind me coming for Thanksgiving?"

"Of course not. You already know Camille and you've met Madison, who owns Morning Jolt. I'm sure you'll love the rest of their friends,"

17

I told Hannah. "Plus, it's just an open house with a brunch buffet, not a sit-down affair, so it'll be totally low key. We just like to get together before everyone goes to their respective families for dinner."

Thanksgiving morning Hannah and I drove across town to the fancy Belltown neighborhood, where Camille's partner Madison lived. She was a tech billionaire but somehow still humble, something that I appreciated about her. She and Camille had been secretly in love with each other for a long time even before a dating app matched them up, forcing them to face to their feelings. Later Madison had purchased Morning Jolt, partly to make sure it wasn't bought up by corporate assholes and partly to get Camille back after they broke up. It worked, they were still together and talking about moving in together.

By the time we got there, the brunch was in full swing. I introduced Hannah to several of the couples in attendance, including Jewel and Alice, Miranda and Elizabeth, Jennifer and Susan, and Elana and Toya, and we met a few women I didn't know. Over the past couple of years this friend group had expanded as more of us had paired up and found love.

Madison's place was festive with a huge buffet set up on one wall, and small seating areas set up around the room. We went to the buffet set up along one wall to fix ourselves a plate of breakfast foods, then sat together on a couch in the corner of the comfortable living room. A uniformed waiter came by and offered us our choice of mimosas or coffee.

"I didn't realize this was a lesbian event...Wait, Camille and Madison are together?" Hannah exclaimed as she nodded to the couple kissing as they waited in line at the buffet.

I looked at her in surprise. "You didn't know? Madison comes in for coffee every morning, doesn't she?"

"Yeah but Camille makes her coffee and gets her a muffin and usually Bob chats with her for a few minutes and then she leaves. I didn't realize they were friends let alone...together."

"Oh yeah, it's a funny story, they had a secret crush on each other for a long time, but they never did anything about it until they were matched up by a lesbian dating app. They've been together ever since."

"What are you gals talking about?" Camille asked as she and Madison came over, balancing plates in their hands and sitting on the love seat across from us. Despite their age gap and different backgrounds, they were cute as hell, and perfect for each other.

"I was just telling Hannah how you got matched up by that dating app."

"Yes, it was scary how accurate it was," Madison explained. "You can't see the person's picture or know their real name until you've been talking for a while, so it really forces you to focus on compatibility instead of superficial things."

"Madison's thinking about trying to buy the app," Camille told us.

"Really?" I asked.

"Yeah, but I don't think they're interested in selling. It's too bad because it would be a nice addition to my company's portfolio."

"Have you signed up on the app yet, Ash?" Camille asked me.

"Not yet. I keep putting it off, I don't know why."

I did know why. Every relationship I had ended badly, and I'd totally given up on love, but there was no way I wanted to bring all that up right now.

"What are you waiting for?" Camille asked. "It's been a while since you dated anyone. Don't you want to find the woman of your dreams and settle down like the rest of us?"

"Woman?" Hannah asked.

"What?"

"She said 'woman' of your dreams," Hannah clarified.

"Yeah, so?"

She seemed surprised, looking at me like she had that first day we'd been roommates when I'd come out in casual clothes, apparently ruining whatever her preconceived notion was about me. That was one thing I'd learned about my new friend: she had a tendency to jump to conclusions based on circumstantial evidence.

"But you were living with a guy before me."

"What about it?"

I was confused why Hannah was looking at me like that. Apparently Madison wasn't though.

"Did you think Ashley was straight or something?" she asked Hannah.

Hannah's cheeks turned red as she realized her error. She waved her hand in my general direction.

"It's just...the pencil skirts, the hair, the guy living in her house, she *seemed* straight, so I assumed the dude was her boyfriend."

I couldn't help it, I started laughing.

"I've never even kissed a man, Hannah, let alone slept with one. I'm as gay as they come."

Hannah

Wow, this changed everything. Or maybe it changed nothing. I was so confused.

Over the last few weeks, I'd spent quite a bit of time with Ashley. We'd fallen into the habit of switching off cooking dinner for each other, and then we'd eat while watching one of the TV shows that we'd discovered we had in common. And when we weren't watching Dexter re-runs or binging on Stranger Things, we would have long conversations about our hopes and dreams.

Never once in those conversations did anything come up that would lead me to believe that Ashley was a lesbian.

In fact, she talked a lot about Brian, the guy who used to live with her, and how he was living with another woman now. I assumed that it was one of those situations where they broke up promising to be friends and the other person was too caught up in their new relationship to keep that promise. I didn't realize they were actually platonic friends.

It certainly made me feel better about the tiny little crush I had on Ashley. I'd told myself a hundred times that I was being ridiculous crushing on the straight girl, but now I wondered if my subconscious was getting lesbian vibes from her or something.

The fact was, I was growing increasingly attracted to her, and when I thought she was straight, I could tell myself that it was impossible to turn someone gay, that it wasn't going to happen. But now that I knew she was a lesbian, there was a glimmer of hope. And I needed to shut that down hard and fast.

I mean really, did my silly heart not remember how only a month ago we'd come home to find ourselves robbed and abandoned by the last woman we thought we'd loved? Besides, Ashley had never shown any indication of being attracted to me anyway. How pathetic could I possibly be?

The answer was...pretty pathetic.

The next couple of weeks I found myself becoming increasingly obsessed with my roommate. It's like now that I knew a relationship with her was theoretically possible, the floodgates had opened. I'd find myself staring at her shapely legs in those conservative little pencil skirts she wore to work. I'd smile when I saw her frowning at the computer when she worked on her book at the dining room table. I'd lay in bed and touch myself while imagining her on the other side of the wall doing the same thing. And every time I'd remind myself: we're just friends, only friends.

That was the other thing: I really liked Ashley as a person. She'd already become one of my best friends. I didn't want to mess that up by doing something stupid like making a pass at her. Besides, Ashley had been talking to some chick on that dating site that Camille and Madison had used.

"You should try it," Ashley told me a few days before Christmas. "It's kind of fun."

"I don't think I'm ready to date," I told her.

I wasn't lying. I was still trying to figure out what had gone wrong with She-Who-Shall-Not-Be-Named. I'd heard from mutual friends that she was with someone else now and that they'd left town, but that's all I knew. They all seemed as surprised about the break-up as I was.

"Hey, do you want to put up a Christmas tree?" Ashley asked me suddenly. "I know it's kind of late, but it might be nice to festive-up the place a little."

"Yeah, that would be nice," I answered. "What do you usually do for Christmas? Go see your family?"

Ashley's face clouded over. "I don't talk to my family. Ever. They kicked me out and disowned me when I came out to them years ago."

Even though society was becoming increasingly more accepting of the LGBTQ population, I knew it still wasn't uncommon for people to have an experience like Ashley's. Many of my friends back in Portland had had similar experiences.

"Aw shit, I'm sorry Ash, that sucks. It's totally their loss."

She blinked a few times, then her expression cleared with what was obviously years of experience hiding her emotions.

"What about you, Hannah? What are your plans for Christmas?"

"I was just going to hang around here. I don't really celebrate Christmas."

"Oh, are you Jewish?"

"I have no idea," I answered. "I grew up in foster care. I don't really remember my parents."

"Didn't you celebrate Christmas with your foster families?" she asked curiously.

"You don't really get holidays in foster care. The state only pays for room and board, so at best you'd maybe get a charity gift or something someone else didn't want."

Even after all these years, I felt a familiar stab of pain in my chest as I remembered being the weird little girl no one wanted, especially at the holidays. You'd think by age thirty-five I'd be over it. I waited for the look of pity I'd come to expect from people when they heard my story, but as usual, Ashley surprised me. Instead of looking sad, her face brightened.

"I've got a great idea!" Ashley said excitedly. "We'll make our own Christmas! We'll wear Santa hats and decorate a tree and make a nice dinner and drink eggnog and watch stupid Christmas movies. It'll be so fun!"

Her enthusiasm was contagious. "You know what, that does sound fun. I'm in."

She jumped up from the table and grabbed a note pad and pen from the counter. "Okay, let's make a list of everything we need."

The following day after work Ashley and I headed to the Christmas tree lot at a local church a few blocks away. That was the great thing about living in this part of the city: everything was close by. We wandered through the lot, debating the pros and cons of each tree as if our lives depended on the decision. With Christmas Eve only a few days away, the trees were pretty well picked over.

"What about this one?" I said, pointing to a tall tree that was a bit scraggly, with one side missing half of its branches.

"That's a Charlie Brown tree," Ashley laughed.

"A what?"

"You know, a Charlie Brown tree, like in the Christmas cartoon."

When I continued to look at her blankly she said, "Have you never seen this? Charlie Brown and Snoopy and the gang get a scraggly Christmas tree because Charlie Brown feels bad for it. It has like three branches but when they give it love, the tree blooms and grows into a beautiful Christmas tree."

I stared at the misshapen tree.

"Oh my God, I'm the Charlie Brown tree," I whispered.

"What?" Ashley asked.

"Nothing. We're getting this tree."

Ashley

I had no idea when I suggested having our own Christmas celebration that it would mean so much to Hannah, but clearly it did. Seeing her face light up was the greatest feeling in the world. Her excitement about picking out a tree had been adorable.

When I was growing up, my family always had a big fancy holiday event, but it had always felt empty. I'd grown up with money but not a lot of love, and when my parents realized that I didn't fit their mold of the perfect future Stepford wife daughter they lost interest in me, even before I'd told them I was gay. I'd come to terms with it long ago, but I hadn't really thought about how they'd sucked the joy out of Christmas for me until I saw how much Hannah was getting into our little celebration.

After we picked up the tree, we borrowed a saw from the building manager and worked together to saw off the bottom of the stump and get the tree set up in a holder with water. We'd spent hours picking out Christmas decorations and ornaments online and did a rush delivery so they would get here in time for us to decorate on Christmas Eve.

I was glad we were going to spend the holiday together. The more time I spent with Hannah the more I liked her. We'd become really good friends during the seven weeks we'd been living together. Usually it took me a while to warm up to someone, but I'd felt comfortable with her immediately. And, if I was honest, I was the tiniest bit attracted to her as well. Well, maybe more than the tiniest bit...

I'd been talking to this woman on a dating app who was an eighty-nine percent compatibility match with me, and for some reason, I kept dragging my feet about meeting her in real life. When I'd finally given in and met her for coffee I'd realized the problem: she wasn't Hannah.

The dating app woman was perfectly nice, but I kept comparing her to Hannah. That's when I realized I would need to hold off on dating until I got these crazy feelings for my roommate under control. Hannah had given me no indication that she had anything but friendly feelings for me and I didn't want to do anything to make her feel uncomfortable, especially when she was renting a room from me.

Christmas Eve was a Saturday and even though Hannah didn't usually work on weekends, she volunteered to take the seven a.m. to four p.m. shift at Morning Jolt so other people could have the day off. I was waiting for her when she got home just after four o'clock. I greeted her at the door wearing jeans, a hideously ugly Christmas sweater, and a jaunty Santa hat on my head.

"Welcome home," I said cheerfully. "The Hannah and Ashley Christmas Celebration starts now!"

I pulled a matching Santa hat out of my back pocket and stepped closer, pulling it over Hannah's straight blue locks. "There you go, that's better."

My eyes dropped to hers and I froze with my hands on the sides of her head. We stared at each other for a moment, her brown eyes widening slightly before I realized I was being a weirdo and stepped back, breaking the spell.

"I made a charcuterie board," I said huskily.

"Ooh, fancy."

"I know, right? I also made eggnog."

While Hannah changed into comfortable clothes I put on a holiday playlist on Spotify, filling the apartment with the festive sounds of winter holidays. It was rare to have a white Christmas in Seattle, but at least we could pretend.

Hannah and I worked together to hang lights on the tree and around the large picture window that looked out into the street.

"I love this," Hannah said as we finished the window. "We should keep the lights up year round."

"I agree. It really brightens the room."

We ate our way through the charcuterie board and drank several glasses of eggnog while we unpackaged the ornaments and decorated the tree. By the time we got to the tinsel, I was feeling a little tipsy.

"I'd better lay off the eggnog for a while," I told Hannah as I playfully tossed a handful of tinsel at her. "Otherwise, I'll pass out before we get to the movie portion of our evening."

We'd decided to have Chinese take-out for dinner, figuring we could eat the leftovers throughout the weekend. Hannah placed the order and we walked together to a restaurant about half a mile away to pick it up. It was a typical winter's night in Seattle: cold and drizzly, but I was glad for the miserable weather. The walk was enough to sober me up by the time we got back to the apartment.

As we walked along the mostly empty streets I kept flashing on that moment earlier when I'd put the Santa hat on Hannah's head. For a minute I'd thought she was going to kiss me. For a minute I thought I was going to kiss her. I shook my head. I needed to put all thoughts of kissing out of my mind before something happened to ruin my friendship with Hannah.

When we got back to our apartment we sat side by side on the couch, boxes of Chinese take-out scattered across the coffee table. I queued up the first in our Christmas movie marathon as Hannah pulled a blanket over our legs to ward off the chill in the living room. We'd turned off all the lights except for the Christmas tree and the lights we'd installed around the front window, leaving the room lit by a soft, almost romantic glow.

"What's first?" Hannah asked.

"Elf."

"I've never seen that."

I rolled my eyes. "You have so much to learn about Christmas, young Hannah."

We spent the next three and a half hours watching "Elf", "A Charlie Brown Christmas", and "Christmas Vacation", laughing and eating and drinking more eggnog until well past midnight.

"Okay, those were all really good," Hannah told me as I turned off the television, leaving the room a little darker without the glow from the screen. "I had a lot of fun tonight."

I turned to face her, noting that her hair looked a little bluer in the glow of the blinking Christmas lights.

"Me too. I'm really glad we're friends."

Hannah shifted, mimicking my position, both of us with one knee bent on the couch and one foot on the floor. The blanket that we were sharing fell to the floor. I realized that we were close enough that only an inch separated our knees on the cushion.

We both lapsed into silence, the air feeling charged around us. We stared at each other for a long, pregnant moment. In the back of my mind, the part of my brain that was still rational was sounding a warning. Unfortunately, that part of my brain was silenced by the part that had drank about a gallon of liberally spiked eggnog.

That part of my brain had no problem urging me to move forward. Apparently Hannah's brain was in full agreement because she met me halfway. Our lips met briefly as we stared into each other's eyes. I felt a jolt that went right from my lips straight to my core.

The kiss turned hot in an instant. We moved closer together, hands coming to each other's shoulders, and I tilted my head to one side as Hannah nipped at my lower lip. I opened for her, and her tongue swooped in, sliding against mine, exploring.

I had the sudden need to get closer and without breaking the kiss I managed to shift until I was kneeling on either side of Hannah's bent leg. The movement brought my breasts against hers, and my nipples hardened painfully against my bra.

My God, this kiss was everything.

The Santa hat slid off my head as Hannah slid her fingers into my hair, tightening in the strands to direct my head, taking control of the kiss. I gripped her shoulders harder and rocked my pussy against her thigh, dry humping her shamelessly.

Just when I was ready to beg her to take me right there on the couch Hannah pulled away, regret clearly written on her face. Damn it, regret was the last thing I wanted to see right now.

"What are we doing, Ashley?" she asked.

Her words were like a bucket of cold water over my head. What were we doing? Hannah was my roommate. One of my best friends. We were both drunk. This was a terrible idea on so many levels.

"I'm so sorry," I said shakily as I moved back. "I don't know came over me."

Hannah grabbed my hand and waited for me to look at her.

"We were both here, Ash," she reminded me. "Look, I really value your friendship and I love being your roommate. We got a little carried away. Let's just forget it happened, okay?"

I nodded. "Sure, we'll forget it ever happened."

As I bid Hannah good night and headed to my bedroom, I knew one thing for sure: I would probably never forget what had happened.

Hannah

How on Earth did I think we could forget what happened? It was the first question that popped into my mind when I opened my eyes in the morning. I was drunk last night, but sadly not drunk enough to forget the feeling of Ashley's soft lips pressed against mine or the way my entire body felt like it lit up when she straddled my thigh.

I sighed deeply as I pulled my sleeping bag over my head. I hoped to God Ashley and I hadn't fucked things up last night. Damn her and her demon eggnog. I knew we shouldn't have drank so much of it.

A soft knock interrupted my ruminations. "Hannah? Are you awake?"

"Yeah, come on in."

"Merry Christmas!" Ashley said brightly. "How would you feel about waffles?"

I groaned. "Aren't you hungover?"

"God yes, that's why I'm making waffles."

I pushed myself to seated. "Will there also be bacon?"

"Of course."

"All right, I'm gonna brush my teeth and I'll be right out."

When I joined Ashley in the kitchen she was midway through cooking breakfast. I poured myself a cup of coffee then set the table, trying to decide if I should bring up the kiss. Maybe Ashley was drunk enough that she forgot it? Any hopes I had about that were dashed as soon as she set the plates down and sat down at the table.

"About the kiss..."

My eyes snapped to Ashley's.

"Yeah?"

She leaned forward, resting her elbows on the table, her beautiful face adorably earnest.

"I have a crazy idea, but hear me out before you say no."

"Um, okay."

"For some time now, I've been increasingly attracted to you, which is quite an inconvenience because I really don't want to be. Attracted to you, I mean."

"You don't?" I couldn't resist asking.

"No, because I like you as a friend and a roommate and if we were to date, when we broke up – which we would inevitably do because, let's face it, neither of us has the best track record – I'd lose not only a great roommate but one of my best friends. And that would really suck. I do not want that to happen."

She took a deep breath.

"I thought it was just me," she continued, "but after last night I realized it was possible, I mean I think it might be true, that you are feeling the same level of attraction towards me that I'm feeling for you, is that right?"

Ashley was incredibly adorable when she was all wound up like this.

"Yeah. I am. And I have the same concerns. I don't want to lose you as a friend or a roommate and as you know, I'm still getting over a bad break-up."

"I have a proposal."

I watched as she took a bite of her bacon and gave me an expectant look, as if I could guess what her proposal was. When she didn't continue I raised my eyebrows at her.

"Well? What's your proposal?"

"I think we should sleep together."

My fork clattered to my plate, sending a piece of waffle flying towards the floor.

"I thought we just agreed it would be a terrible idea to sleep with each other," I reminded her.

She shook her head. "It would be a terrible idea to date, or to get emotionally involved in any way. But what if we just slept together once to get it out of our systems?"

I looked around the kitchen. "Am I living in a TV rom com right now?"

She rolled her eyes. "To be blunt, I think we're both just horny. But because we both have had a string of bad relationships, we're turning our horniness towards each other because we're safe. If we sleep together once we'll clear the pipes so to speak, so we can focus on finding people to date instead of misplacing our attraction on each other."

"And when would this happen, exactly?"

"Tonight. One night only."

I frowned and pointed a piece of bacon at her as I replayed her words. "One time or one night? You said both."

"Isn't it the same thing?"

"Uh, no. You can have sex more than once a night, as I'm sure you know."

"Okay, one night, that'll give us one orgasm each."

"Why limit ourselves to one orgasm?" I asked curiously.

For the first time Ashley seemed the tiniest bit embarrassed by our conversation.

"Well, it's not like most people are multi-orgasmic."

"They're not?"

"No." Her voice sounded a bit unsure.

"You've never had more than one orgasm in a night?" I clarified.

She shook her head, a flush rising up her pale cheeks. "No, it takes me a while to, um, get to the finish line and after that, my body's done. Even when I'm alone I'm a one and done kind of gal."

"Hmm, that sounds like a challenge to me. But why one night?" I asked. "Why not be friends with benefits? Theoretically I mean?"

"It's too high a risk," she explained. "One of us might catch feelings and then the whole system is ruined. We just need to bang it out, then we can go back to our easy, uncomplicated friendship and get out there and find some women to date who aren't us."

"This is either the most ridiculously stupid plan ever, or the most ridiculously brilliant, I can't decide which."

Ashley gave me the confident smile that I loved, her previous embarrassment gone.

"It's brilliant Hannah. Now finish your breakfast and give it some thought. If we're going to do this I want to wait until later anyway. I have plans for us today."

After we ate, Ashley and I went to the living room to open our Christmas presents. Last night we'd each put a couple of presents under the tree for each other and while I'd been sleeping Ashley had hung two stockings on the wall under the window, one with each of our names. They were bulging with candies, gum, and trinkets like pens, ponytail holders, and stickers. I was ridiculously excited about it. I'd never had a stocking before.

"You made yourself a stocking too?" I laughed.

"Of course not, those are from Santa," Ashley said archly.

"Well Santa has good taste," I mumbled as I shoved a sucker in my mouth. "I love a Tootsie Pop."

Ashley opened her presents first, oohing and ahhing over the Stranger Things pajamas, vanilla bath bombs, and new earbuds I got her. We laughed as I opened my first gift from Ashley, a Stranger Things tee shirt.

"Great minds think alike," I said happily.

Then she slid a large package over to me. I ripped the wrapping paper off and, to my absolute horror, for the first time in thirty years, my eyes filled with tears.

Ashley

"You don't like it?" I asked in alarm. "We can totally take that back to the store and get you something else."

"No," Hannah sniffed, hugging the 'bed in a bag' set to her chest like she thought I'd take it away from her. "I love it, really. I love it so much."

"I don't understand. No judgement or anything, but I noticed you were using a sleeping bag instead of sheets, so I figured She-Who-Shall-Not-Be-Named swiped your sheets and blankets when she took off."

Hannah unzipped the plastic bag, removing the blue sheets and pillowcases and the multicolored geometric patterned comforter. When I'd seen it, the color of the sheets reminded me of her hair.

"I've just, well, I've never had new sheets or a new comforter. When you're in foster care you get all the hand-me-downs."

Her voice as small and sad, making me frown.

"You're thirty-five years old. You've been out of foster care for what, seventeen years? What have you been doing for sheets since then?"

"I usually get them from the Goodwill or garage sales."

I flashed back to the day she'd told me that she'd gotten a new bed from a neighbor who was moving out and planning to put the bed in the dumpster. She'd probably still be sleeping on that air mattress if the guy hadn't tossed his old bed.

Suddenly I was annoyed with my friend. I'd already noticed her penchant for thrift store shopping and dumpster diving, but now I was realizing that her desire to save money had more to do with self-esteem than budgeting.

"Hannah!" I said sternly. "Just because you had nothing when you were a kid doesn't mean you have to act like that now. You're stuck in a scarcity mindset, like you think you can't have anything nice, or you don't deserve it or something. I got that bed in a bag for sixty-nine ninety-nine at Macy's. I'm pretty sure you could have spent seventy bucks on yourself at some point in your adult life, you spend more than that dying your hair. You've been living here for six or seven weeks now, working, making tips, and you couldn't even pick up some nineteen ninety-nine sheets from a department store or something? Stop living like you have nothing, damn it!"

Her mouth dropped open in shock, but I wasn't sure if it was because my words were striking a chord or because she'd never seen me angry before. And I was angry. Hannah was so kind and generous to everyone – everyone except herself. No wonder her previous girlfriends had walked all over her. She didn't believe she deserved better, and neither did they.

When I stopped ranting she stared at me for what felt like an hour before she said, "Are you done?"

"Yeah."

"You look really hot when you're angry. I've decided that I want to put these fancy new sheets on my bed and spend the rest of the day, as you so eloquently suggested earlier, banging it out and getting each other out of our systems."

My breath caught in my chest as she continued. "I also plan to show you that it is absolutely possible to come more than once a day."

"But it's still morning," I squeaked, suddenly nervous. As much as I wanted Hannah, I didn't actually believe she would agree to my crazy proposal.

"You can't have morning sex?" she asked with a smirk.

She gently set her comforter down on top of its bag as if it was her most precious possession, and pushed herself to her hands and knees, crawling across the floor towards me. I glanced down, taking in the way her breasts gently swayed from side to side, confirming that she wasn't wearing a bra under the sweatshirt that she'd slept in.

I licked my lips. I'd always been a breast woman.

Hannah kept crawling towards me and over my lap. I leaned backwards until my back met the floor. She gave me a smile that was downright predatory, then lowered her curvy body on top of mine, one elbow on either side of my head.

"You're fucking beautiful, do you know that?"

Before I could answer she lowered her head, taking my lips in a kiss that felt like a claiming. I sighed against her, and she slipped her tongue inside my mouth, exploring. I reached up to wrap my arms around her back, sliding my palms up and down the soft fabric of her ancient sweatshirt. I felt simultaneously excited and relaxed, it was the weirdest feeling.

Hannah kissed me long and leisurely, slowly amping up the pleasure in a way that I'd never experienced before. I'd had more than a handful of lovers in my life, and kissing had always felt like a means to an end. With Hannah, it felt like a sensual act all its own.

I worked my legs out from underneath hers so I could hug one of her muscular thighs between mine, shamelessly pumping up against her, desperate to get some pressure against my clit. Meanwhile Hannah continued to make love to my mouth, occasionally breaking away to allow us to catch our breath while she peppered little kisses along my jaw.

Finally – finally – when I felt ready to come just from kissing and dry humping her leg, Hannah slid off my body and unbuttoned my flannel pajama top. She pulled one arm up over my head, then the other, but to my surprise she didn't pull the top all the way off. Instead, she used the sleeves wrapped around my wrists to secure my hands together above my head. I tugged against my pajama top, but between the knots she'd made, and the shirt fabric trapped underneath my back, it didn't budge.

Hannah lifted one eyebrow at my actions but didn't say a word. Instead, she moved down to capture one breast in her mouth. I'd had lovers suck on my nipples of course, but Hannah consumed my whole breast, sucking as much as she could into the moist heat of her mouth, sucking hard while her hand came up to flick at the nipple of my other breast.

"Hannah!" I gasped.

She released my breast with a pop, licking her way down to circle my belly button, then shifting to her knees so she could pull my pajama bottoms and panties down my legs. Hannah stared at my pussy like it was the best thing she'd ever seen. I squirmed under her perusal, pulling at my bound wrists.

"Open for me, baby," she said softly.

I widened my legs and she slid between them on her stomach. I was already so primed I damn near came just from the breath of air she exhaled over my mound. Hannah used her fingers to spread my lower lips, then licked my slit from bottom to top.

"You're so wet already," she said with obvious satisfaction.

Her tongue came up to circle my clit, coming close to where I needed her, but never quite making contact. Again and again she circled, and when I lifted my pelvis trying to get her where I needed her, she clamped her hands down on my hips, holding me still so she could continue to tease me.

"Hannah, please!" I whined

She looked up and met my eyes.

"Tell me what you want, Ashley. Use your words."

I huffed out a frustrated breath. "I want you to make me come. Please."

"Okay."

When she lowered her head again, she honed right in on my clit, flicking it back and forth with her tongue until I was right on the edge. Then she sucked the swollen bundle of nerves into her mouth, closed her lips around me, and bit down gently.

Fire raced through my veins, and I moaned loudly as my orgasm hit me. My back bowed off the floor, my bound wrists pounding uselessly against the floor over my head as I rode the waves of my release, Hannah licking and sucking on my clit until I finally started to come down.

And when it was over, I knew instinctively I would never be the same again.

Hannah

Holy shit, Ashley losing control was the most beautiful thing I'd ever seen. Her small breasts bounced with every heaving breath and the arms that I'd bound above her head shook.

I pushed up to my knees and took my time enjoying the view, from her heart shaped face to her still-perky breasts, down to the indent of her small waist, the softness of her belly, and the narrow curve of her hips. Her pussy was waxed other than a small patch of hair at her apex, and she had a thigh gap between her slim but shapely thighs. I realized with a start she was still wearing wool socks, the only piece of clothing she had left on. It made me smile.

When she'd finally caught her breath, I bent Ashley's knees, placing her feet on the floor, her thighs on either side of mine as I kneeled between her legs.

"What are you doing?"

She seemed a bit dazed. I loved that I'd had that effect on her. Ashley was normally so put together, so in control. Seeing her like this was a gift.

"Proving you wrong."

"Huh?"

I couldn't help but feel a bit proud that I'd fucked her senseless on the first try.

"Remember you challenged me to prove that you're not multi-orgasmic."

She lifted her head. "I did no such thing."

"Sure you did."

I slid my finger between her dripping pussy lips. "We're going to test that theory now."

"But…"

"Shhh….just lie back and enjoy it."

My finger slid into her channel, and I began pumping in and out, starting slow and picking up speed as I went along. I watched Ashley's face carefully, monitoring her reactions, gauging which motions seemed to bring her the most pleasure.

After a few moments I added a second finger, separating them inside her to stretch her a bit. She was shockingly tight. Ashley made a little keening noise as I resumed the thrusting into her channel, a little rougher now. She was already primed from her first orgasm, so it didn't take long before she was bracing her feet against the floor and lifting her hips to meet my questing fingers.

"That feels so good," she said quietly. "Keep doing that."

I smiled and slid in a third finger, filling her up and pushing as deep as I could go. With every thrust the heel of my hand rubbed hard against her already-sensitive clit. When I felt her internal muscles start to quiver I moved my other hand to her clit and pinched it sharply between my fingers. At the same time, I curved the fingers inside her channel, aiming for her G-spot.

"Be a good girl and come for me again, Ashley."

I wasn't sure which of my actions set her off, maybe all of them, but less than thirty seconds later Ashley was breaking apart beneath me again, shaking and shuddering. This orgasm seemed deeper, less controlled. Her beautiful face was contorted in a look that was a cross between pain and ecstasy as she mumbled my name over and over again.

When she was done she sagged back to the floor, then gasped as she watched me remove my fingers from her pussy and put them into my mouth, licking them clean.

"Delicious," I said, giving her a wicked smile.

"I'm dying," she moaned. "You've fucking killed me."

I crawled around her and untied her wrists, then shifted to lay on the floor by her side, throwing my arm around her waist and resting my head on her shoulder. Ashley brought her arms down, wrapping one around my shoulders, and placing the other on top of the arm on her stomach.

"What was that you were saying earlier about people only being able to have one orgasm a night?" I asked smugly. "Because I'm pretty sure you just had two in less than an hour."

"Fine, I concede to your superior orgasm giving skills," she panted. "You really should give a class."

"That'd be one way to make money," I joked.

"When I regain control of my limbs," she said, "We are going to put those new sheets on your bed and then I'm going to show you this thing I can do with my tongue. All the girls love it."

"I like the way you think, Ash. I mean, if we only have one day, we'd better make the most of it right? Make sure we are well and truly out of each other's systems?"

I ignored the pit of nausea in my stomach as I said that.

And I pretended not to notice that Ashley's voice sounded almost sad when she responded, "Right. One day. That's the plan."

But by the time we were ready to move again, by some unspoken agreement we decided to save round two for later. What had happened was so intense, we needed a breather. Plus, we'd worked hard to plan what we'd deemed the perfect Christmas Day schedule and I think neither of us wanted to give that up, even for incredible sex.

We both got dressed in comfortable clothes and our goofy Christmas hats, turned on the Christmas tree lights, and spent the next few hours watching Christmas movies. For today's line-up Ashley had chosen "A Christmas Story", "Bad Santa", and several old cartoon type shows including "Rudolph the Red-Nosed Reindeer", "Frosty the Snowman", and "Santa Claus is Coming to Town".

At some point we made a huge bowl of popcorn and mixed it with a bag of M&Ms – something that I'd never tried before I lived with Ashley – and we snacked on the mixture and shared a six-pack of a special Christmas brew IPA from the brewery we'd visited the first day we'd been roommates.

When darkness fell we heated up the pre-cooked dinner we'd picked up from the store and ate a Christmas ham with scalloped potatoes, buttered green beans, biscuits, and salad. After dinner we played cards by the Christmas tree while listening to Christmas music on Spotify. It was corny and fun. Then we put those new sheets on my bed, and I rode Ashley's face until I damn near passed out as I came all over her talented tongue. And when it was over, we fell asleep, wrapped up in each other's arms.

It was the perfect day, easily the best Christmas that I'd ever had.

Honestly, I'd mostly avoided celebrating Christmas as an adult, wanting to avoid the disappointment I remembered as a child. As I enjoyed my day with Ashley I realized that I'd been short-sighted. As an adult I had the autonomy to make Christmas be whatever I wanted, to create my own vision of a perfect day, just like Ashley and I had done today.

Ashley had been right when she gave me that little speech earlier. I'd been living my life from a scarcity mode, always telling myself I didn't deserve more than crumbs. I never bought myself anything new, always telling myself that resale was just as good. I'd never asked for anything in my relationships. Back in Portland all of my friends, all of my girlfriends, even my employers had taken advantage of me. And I let them, because I never stood up for myself, never believed I deserved to come first.

Even this agreement to have one night only with Ashley was crumbs. Because the truth was, I was head over heels in love with my roommate. I'd been in love with her before I'd made her come – twice – earlier today. I fell a little bit more in love with her after she made me come, and a little more still as we snuggled together on my brand new sheets and talked quietly until we both fell into a deep, peaceful sleep.

She'd told me not to accept less than I deserved. Well, I deserved Ashley. I just needed to figure out a way to convince her of that. She had her own demons, but after what had happened on the living room floor earlier today, and again in my bed, I had no doubt in my mind that her feelings for me ran as deep as mine did for her.

At least I hoped they did...

Ashley

"All right, out with it. What's going on?"

I looked up as my best friend Brian came into the room, his "don't mess with me" face firmly in place. I looked behind him. "Where's Amy?"

"She went out with her sister so we could talk privately."

"You didn't have to kick her out," I protested.

"Yes I did," he said. "I couldn't take any more of this moping. And it was clear I wasn't going to get the truth out of you with anyone else here."

He swiped my legs off the couch so he could sit on the other side facing me. "Now quit stalling Ash. Tell me what's wrong."

"Nothing's wrong," I lied, refusing to meet his eyes.

He pinned me with a hard stare.

"Are you forgetting who you're talking to?" he asked. "I've known you since you were thirteen. Something's wrong. You showed up here three days ago for an unplanned and unannounced visit…"

"You said I should visit any time," I interrupted. "You said I didn't need an invitation."

Brian ignored me, continuing, "You showed up on my doorstep looking like the weight of the world is on your shoulders and since then, you've spent most of the time staring into space like a teenager with a crush. I haven't seen you this discombobulated since you came out to your parents. What happened?"

Brian had been my best friend since we were freshman in high school. He'd been the first person I'd come out to when I realized I had a crush on Angela Bowman in tenth grade. He'd not been surprised that I was a lesbian, which showed how well he knew me. When I came out to my parents right after high school graduation they'd kicked me out and Brian's parents had let me stay with them for the summer before I went to college, and every college break after that.

Brian and I had been through a lot together, including the ups and downs of our love lives. He'd finally found the perfect woman. Amy was strong and sweet and treated him well and I loved them together, but I'd also been devastated when Amy got a promotion that required her to move an hour away from Seattle. Brian had gone with her, since he worked from home and it didn't matter where he lived, but I hated that for the first time in over twenty years I couldn't see Brian every day.

My best friend watched me patiently, letting me process my thoughts before I spoke.

"I did something stupid!" I finally blurted out. "I slept with my new roommate."

One corner of Brian's mouth quirked up. "I wondered how long that was going to take."

I frowned. "What does that mean?"

"It was obvious that you are totally into her. You were all," he raised his voice in an obvious attempt at imitating me. "*Hannah is so cool, Hannah is so pretty, Hannah is so funny, did I tell you what Hannah said?*"

I kicked him in the leg with my foot. "I don't sound like that."

"So what's the problem? Was the sex bad?"

"No, it was the best sex I ever had," I said miserably.

"Oh, so she's not into you as much as you're into her?" he asked sympathetically.

"I have no idea how she feels about me."

He frowned. "What?"

"We had a perfect day, and I had two orgasms in an hour for the first time ever, and we watched Christmas movies and cooked together and had so much fun but then I got freaked out about the agreement and left before she woke up."

"Wait. Rewind. I'm totally confused."

I brought my knees to my chest and rested my chin on them.

"I was getting more and more obsessed with her, you know, like she'd come out in these ratty old sweats with stains on them and I'd think it was the sexiest thing I'd ever seen."

Brian nodded. "Yeah, Amy has this tattered sweatshirt that's hotter than any lingerie I swear."

"We'd decided to spend Christmas together as you know, and we had too much eggnog and we accidentally kissed."

"Accidentally? What, like you both tripped and your lips fell into each other?"

I rolled my eyes.

"It was an incredible kiss and it proved that we were both attracted to each other. When I sobered up, I had what I thought was this great idea, we should just have one night together, you know, to get it out of our systems."

Brian rolled his eyes. "You're an idiot. That never works. Everybody knows that."

I ignored him and kept going with my story.

"It turned out she was totally into it – sleeping together—and like I said, we had the perfect Christmas day and we, um, you know, several times and it was good. Incredible. The best. But then I woke up in her arms and I imagined her being all casual and saying, 'okay great I'm glad we got this out of our systems' and us trying to go back to how things were."

I took a deep, shuddering breath.

"That's when I realized that I'd fallen in love with her. So I left her a note that I was coming to visit you for a few days, and I'd see her later."

Brian ran his hand through his thick hair. "Jesus Christ you're an idiot. You know falling in love with someone is a good thing, right?"

"Only if it's reciprocated." My voice was small.

"You didn't give her a chance to reciprocate," he bellowed. "And didn't you tell me that her last girlfriend ditched her when she wasn't home? Now you ditched her while she was sleeping? Did it not occur to you that this probably feels like the same thing if she has feelings for you, which she probably does?"

My eyes widened. "Oh crap."

"Look Ash, I know your parents did a number on you and taught you that love is conditional, and your string of crappy girlfriends didn't help, but you're thirty-fucking-five years old now. Grow up and have a big girl relationship."

Brian gave me a long look, then continued, "I've never seen you so happy or so obviously smitten with someone like you've been with Hannah, nor have I seen you so upset about the idea of losing any of the assorted losers you've dated in the past. You need to make things right with this girl before you lose your chance to have what I have with Amy. And believe me, you do not want to lose that chance. I wouldn't trade a relationship based on true love for anything Ashley, and nothing would make me happier than for you to have that too. Now get the fuck out of my house and go home to make things right with your girl."

Hannah

"See you tomorrow."

I waved at Camille as we exited the coffee shop, then headed toward the apartment I shared with Ashley, my feet like lead. I was trying not to panic, but I knew something was wrong. I'd woken up alone the day after Christmas with only a hastily scribbled note from Ashley on the kitchen table.

"Hey, I'm heading up to visit Brian for a few days. Talk to you later, A."

She'd never mentioned visiting Brian, in fact, we'd talked about possibly going for a hike the day after Christmas if the weather was good. And when I'd poked my head into her bedroom it had been unusually messy, with drawers pulled out and clothes on the floor as if she'd packed in a hurry. It was so reminiscent of my ex leaving me it made my chest hurt. Although at least Ashley hadn't robbed me. Unless you counted my stolen heart.

I also hadn't heard a peep from her the entire time she'd been gone. Even though we lived together, we usually texted each other once or twice during the day. Hell, sometimes we texted each other from other rooms of the apartment. But my phone had been silent the entire time she'd been gone. Clearly she regretted sleeping with me.

What was it about me that made people not want me? My whole life story was about being the person no one wanted to keep

I'd thought things were going great with Ashley. Too great. Maybe she could tell that I was in love with her and thought I was somehow being too clingy? I mean, I didn't think I was being clingy. But it was suspect that just when I'd decided to pursue her she'd disappeared. Damn it. Whatever was wrong, I just wished she would have talked to me about it. I thought we had a better relationship than for her to just ghost me like that.

I sighed as I stuck my key into the lock. I wasn't looking forward to another night alone.

"Hey."

I heard Ashley's voice as soon as I opened the door to the apartment. She was standing in the foyer, with a look on her face that I couldn't interpret. She had smudges under her eyes, as if she hadn't been sleeping. I knew the feeling.

Play it cool Hannah, I told myself. *Don't be a clingy loser. She clearly wants to stick to the one night only agreement, that's why she took off.*

"Oh hey Ash, how was your trip?" I kept my voice casual as I walked past her, hanging my coat on the rack.

"Fine."

"Great."

I headed into the kitchen for a bottle of water, realizing that Ashley had followed me into the room. I met her gaze for a moment and when she didn't say anything, I started to move past her again, but she grabbed my wrist, stopping my progress.

"I'm sorry," she said softly.

"For what?"

"For running off like that."

I pulled my wrist away. "Hey no problem, I know you really miss seeing Brian."

I started walking again and she called after me. "I didn't leave because I missed Brian, it was because I was scared."

Her words stopped me in my tracks. I turned around slowly and looked at her. "Scared of what?"

"Remember I said I just wanted us to sleep together once and get it out of our systems?" she asked.

That burning pain was back in my chest. "Yeah Ash, I remember. Don't worry, I won't renege on our agreement if that's what you're scared of."

"I'm not scared you'll renege, I'm scared you won't."

"Huh?"

She stepped closer to me, taking both of my hands in hers. My eyes flew to meet her gaze, her eyes look wide and vulnerable.

"I'm just going to put this out there and hope I'm not making a fool of myself. I've fallen in love with you, Hannah."

"You're in love with me?" I asked in confusion.

Her eyes flashed with pain. "Yeah, I mean, I don't want to make you feel uncomfortable and you don't have to say it back or anything, I just wanted to let you know how I feel."

"No one's ever told me they loved me before," I said in shock.

"Well, now you know," she said primly, starting to pull away.

"Say it again," I demanded. "I want to make sure I wasn't imagining it."

She rolled her eyes. "I love you, Hannah."

"I love you too, Ashley."

"You're not just saying that to make me feel better, are you?" she asked.

"I realized it after you fell asleep the other night and I was planning to tell you after we woke up, but then you were gone."

"Really?" Her eyes welled with tears.

"Yeah."

"Well, aren't we just the fucked up couple?"

"Are we going to be a couple now?" I confirmed.

"We sure are."

"Well, the good thing is that we started as friends, so we have a good base even if we are a little fucked up. And we both have a lot of experience in terrible relationships and know what we don't want. So if we just do the opposite of what's happened in our other relationships, we should be totally fine."

Ashley tilted her head as she considered my words. "You know what? That actually makes sense in a weird way."

"Of course it does." I tugged her hands, pulling her until the front of her body connected with mine. "How about we seal our new relationship status with a kiss?" I asked.

Ashley lifted on her toes, bringing her lips close to mine. "I got a better idea," she said as she pressed a quick kiss on my lips.

"What's that?"

"Let's take this reunion into the bedroom."

She grabbed my hand, leading me to her bedroom, and by unspoken agreement, we both removed our clothes. We flew towards each other in a mash of lips and teeth, kissing as if our lives depended on it.

We transitioned onto the bed, Ashley laying on top of me before moving downwards, kissing her way down my neck to my breasts, my belly, and finally my pussy. By the time she got there, I was dripping wet.

"Mmm," she made a sound of approval as she licked up my seam. I bent my knees, opening them out to the side to give her more access and she licked me again and again until I was thrashing beneath her.

My fingers curled in her hair, directing her where I wanted her most, and she concentrated her attention on my clit, circling it with maddening slowness. Ashley shifted so she could slide her finger into my channel, pumping in and out a few times before adding a second finger. Meanwhile her tongue moved faster and harder on my clit until it was almost too much.

"Ash!" I gasped. "I, it's…"

I couldn't form words, but it didn't matter because she bent her fingers just then, hitting the spot inside me that made my orgasm crash through me so hard that my breath left my body in a whoosh and my vision grew fuzzy as my spine jackknifed off the bed.

My whole body was consumed by the orgasm. I had no control of my limbs, no control of the gibberish coming out of my mouth, I just gave myself over to the pleasure until I finally sagged down to the bed, completely spent.

Ashley grabbed the blanket from the bottom of the bed, pulling it over me and coming up to lay down next to me. She giggled. "You should see your face. You look like you saw God or something."

I was too exhausted to turn my head, so I just moved my eyes in her direction. "I think I might have."

She hugged me close.

"I love you Hannah."

"I love you too. And I promise I'll return the favor and make you come too, maybe even a few times, as soon as I can move my body again."

Epilogue – Ashley

Three years later...

"She hit me!"

"She hit me first!"

"Why did we think this was a good idea?" Hannah asked me as the two angry little girls came racing up to us.

"You wanted to help kids like you, remember?"

Six months after Hannah and I had gotten back together we'd gotten married. Hannah had been promoted to manager of Morning Jolt after Bob retired and between our two jobs and my writing income, we'd had enough money to buy a little house. Last Christmas we'd gotten the idea to apply to be foster parents. Hannah had been nostalgic, thinking of all the holidays when she'd felt alone and forgotten. And while being foster parents was rewarding, it was also hard.

Case in point: these two sisters who hadn't stopped trying to kill each other since they'd gotten here.

"Hey girls," I said softly but firmly. "We've got a surprise for you."

They both quieted immediately.

"A surprise?" Jasmine, the oldest girl, spoke first, her voice cautious. "For us?"

"Yes, for you. Come with us," Hannah said with a small smile.

I took Jasmine's hand and Hannah took Eliza's hand as we led them to the family room. Hannah opened the double doors with a flourish, revealing the large Christmas tree that we'd kept hidden from the kids in the three days they'd been here. It was fully decorated and lit up brightly, and we'd hung lights around the windows and along the fireplace mantle.

"Wow," Eliza said, her voice awestruck. "It's beautiful."

"Today's Christmas Eve," Hannah said. "We are going to have a nice dinner and then you each get to open one present before Santa comes."

"Santa doesn't come to foster kids," Jasmine said bitterly.

"He does here," Hannah said. "Just you wait, we already talked to him and made sure that he added you two to his list. Now go look through the packages with your name on them and pick one for tonight."

As the excited girls shook and examined every package under the tree I pulled my wife in close to my side and gave her a big squeeze.

"Merry Christmas," I whispered into her ear.

She shivered.

"I've got a Christmas surprise for you later. In the bedroom."

Her smile lit up her face.

"I can't wait. I hope it's new sheets."

***

If you liked this book, please consider leaving a review or rating on my author page to let me know.

Want to read about how Camille and Madison met and fell in love? Read "My Secret Crush[1]", available everywhere now.

And check out the next book in the Friends to Lovers series, "My Valentine's Gift[2]", coming in February 2023.

Don't forget to join my newsletter and receive a copy of my book "Hotel Spanking" for free. My newsletter subscribers are the first to hear about all of my new releases and sales. Go to bit.ly/rebabooks ***for more information.***

Be sure to keep reading for a free preview from the first book in Reba Bale's "Friends to Lovers" series, available now on all major retailers.

---

1. https://books2read.com/u/mVAR5r

2. https://books2read.com/MyValGift

Special Preview

The Divorcee's First Time
The Friends to Lovers Series Book 1
By Reba Bale

"It's done," I said triumphantly. "My divorce is final."

My best friend Susan paused in the process of sliding into the restaurant booth, her sharply manicured eyebrows raising almost to her hairline. "Dickhead finally signed the papers?" she asked, her tone hopeful.

I nodded as Susan settled into the seat across from me. "The judge signed off on it today. Apparently his barely legal girlfriend is knocked up, and she wants to get a ring on her finger before the big event." I explained with a touch of irony in my voice. "The child bride finally got it done for me."

Susan smiled and nodded. "Well congratulations and good riddance. Let's order some wine."

We were most of the way through our second bottle when the conversation turned back to my ex. "I wonder if Dickhead and his Child Bride will last for the long haul," Susan mused.

I shook my head and blew a chunk of hair away from my mouth.

"I doubt it," I told her. "Someday she's gonna roll over and think, there's got to be something better out there than a self-absorbed man child who doesn't know a clitoris from a doorknob."

Susan laughed, sputtering her wine. I eyed her across the table. Although she was ten years older than me, we had been best friends for the last five years. We worked together at the accounting firm. She had been my trainer when I first came there, fresh out of school with my degree. We bonded over work, but soon realized that we were kindred spirits.

Susan was rapidly approaching forty but could easily pass for my age. Her hair was black and shiny, hinting at her Puerto Rican heritage, with blunt bangs and blond highlights that she paid a fortune for. Her face was clear and unlined, with large brown eyes and cheek bones that could cut glass. She was an avid runner and worked hard to maintain a slim physique since the women in her family ran towards the chunkier side.

I was almost her complete opposite. Blonde curls to her straight dark hair, blue eyes instead of brown, curvy where she was lean, introverted to her extrovert.

But somehow, we clicked. We were closer than sisters. Honestly, I don't know how I would have gotten through the last year without her. She had been the first one I called when my marriage fell apart, and she had supported me throughout the whole process.

It had been a big shock when I came home early one day and found my husband getting a blow job in the middle of our living room. It had been even more shocking when I saw the fresh young face at the other end of that blow job.

"What the fuck are you doing?" I had screeched, startling them both out of their sex stupor. "You're getting blow jobs from children now?"

The girl had looked up from her knees with eyes glowing in righteous indignation. "I'm not a child, I'm 19," she had informed me proudly. "I'm glad you finally found out. I give him what you don't, and he loves me."

I looked into the familiar eyes of my husband and saw the panic and confusion there. I made it easy for him. "Get out," I told him firmly, my voice leaving no room for argument. "Take your teenage girlfriend and get the fuck out. We're getting a divorce. Expect to hear from my lawyer."

The condo was in my name. I had purchased it before we were married, and since I had never added his name to the deed, he had no rights to it. There was no question he would be the one leaving.

My husband just stared at me with his jaw hanging open like he couldn't believe it. "But Jennifer," he whined. "You don't understand. Let me explain."

"There's nothing to understand," I told him sadly. "This is a deal breaker for me, and you know that as well as I do. We are done."

The girl had taken his hand and smiled triumphantly. "Come on baby," she told him. "Zip up and let's get out of here. We can finally be together like we planned."

"Yeah baby," I had sneered. "I'll box up your stuff. It'll be in the hallway tomorrow. Pick it up by 6:00 o'clock or I'm trashing it all."

After they left my first call was to the locksmith, but my second call was to Susan.

That night was the last time I had seen my husband until we had met for the court-ordered pre-divorce mediation. He spent most of that session reiterating what he had told me in numerous voice mails, emails and sessions spent yelling on the other side of my front door. He loved me. He had made a terrible mistake. He wasn't going to sign the papers. We were meant to be together. Needless to say, mediation hadn't been very successful. Fortunately, I had been careful to keep our assets separate, as if I knew that someday I would be in this situation.

Through it all, Susan had been my rock. In the end I don't think I was even that sad about the divorce, I was really angrier with myself for staying in a relationship that wasn't fulfilling with a man I didn't love anymore.

"You need to get some quality sex." Susan drew my attention back to the present. "Bang him out of your system."

"I don't know," I answered slowly. "I think I need a hiatus."

"A hiatus from what?" Susan asked with a frown. "You haven't had sex in what, 18 months?"

I nodded. "Yeah, but I just can't take a disappointing fumble right now. I would rather have nothing than another three-pump chump."

I shook my head and continued, "I'm going to stick with my battery-operated boyfriend, he never disappoints me."

Susan smiled. "That's because you know your way around your own vajayjay."

She motioned to the waiter to bring us a third bottle of wine.

"That's why I like to date women," she continued. "We already know our way around the equipment."

I nodded thoughtfully. "You make a good point."

Susan leaned forward. "We've never talked about this," she said earnestly. "Have you ever been with a woman?"

For more of the story, check out "The Divorcee's First Time" by Reba Bale, available for immediate purchase on your favorite retail sites[1] today.

***

Want a free book? Join my newsletter and receive a free copy of my book "Hotel Spanking" for free. I promise I will only email you when there are new releases or special sales, so go to bit.ly/rebabooks and sign up today.

---

1.   https://books2read.com/u/bpznKX

Other Books by Reba Bale

Check out my other books, available on most major online retailers now. Go to my webpage[1] to learn more.

Friends to Lovers Series

The Divorcee's First Time

My BFF's Sister

My Rockstar Assistant

My College Crush

My Fake Girlfriend

My Secret Crush

My Holiday Love

My Valentine's Gift

Unlikely Doms Series

Alpha in a Sweater Vest

Alpha Plumber

Hotel Spanking

Alpha Student

Alpha Yogi

The Voyeur Romance Series

Naughty Sunbathing

Naughty Dinner Date

Naughty Laundry Date

Naughty Camping

The Spanking Therapy Series

The Reluctant Bride's First Spanking

The Reluctant Bride Gets Caught

The Billionaire Gets Punished

The Divorce Recovery Series

Spanking Justice: A Middle-Aged Divorcee's First Spanking

---

1. https://books2read.com/ap/nB2qJv/Reba-Bale

A Punishing Workout: Spanked by the Trainer
A Disciplined Budget: Spanked by the Accountant
The Curvy Reporter Gets Punished

Paying for Tuition

The Babysitter's Ride Home
The Babysitter's First Menage
The Teaching Assistant's Lesson
The Billionaire's Assistant

The Marriage Survival Series

Finding His Alpha: A Wife's First Spanking
Watching His Wife: The First Time Sharing
Exploring His Fantasy: A First Time Gay Ménage

Toys for Grown-Ups Series

Financial Punishment
Menage a Geek

Punishing Holidays

Turkey and a Spanking
Shopping and a Spanking

Standalone Hotwife Romances

Hotwife in the Woods
Hotwife on the Beach
Hotwife Under the Tree

Standalone Menage Romances

Pie Promises
Tornado Warning
Summer in Paradise

Standalones

The Ride of My Life
Taken by Surprise
Share Me: A Cheating Husband's Punishment

Want a free book? Join my newsletter and receive a free copy of my book "Hotel Spanking" for free. I promise I will only email you when there are new releases or special sales, so go to bit.ly/rebabooks and sign up today.

About the Author

Reba Bale loves writing naughty stories where the characters are able to tap into their inner fantasies and experience spanking, bondage, humiliation, or other activities on the non-vanilla side of life. When Reba is not writing she is reading the same naughty stories she likes to write.

You can follow Reba on Twitter,[2] Instagram[3], or visit her webpage at bit.ly/AuthorRebaBale[4].

Be sure to follow Reba on your favorite retailer and sign up for her newsletter[5] at bit.ly/rebabooks so you are first to hear about all the new releases.

---

2. https://twitter.com/AuthorRebaBale

3. https://www.instagram.com/author_reba_bale/

4. https://bit.ly/AuthorRebaBale

5. https://storyoriginapp.com/giveaways/ff4a004c-e434-11ea-9482-b3f353fcff13

Don't miss out!

Visit the website below and you can sign up to receive emails whenever Reba Bale publishes a new book. There's no charge and no obligation.

https://books2read.com/r/B-A-IDTM-ITNDC

BOOKS2READ

Connecting independent readers to independent writers.

Did you love *My Holiday Love*? Then you should read *The Divorcee's First Time: A Hot Friends-to-Lovers Lesbian Romance*[6] by Reba Bale!

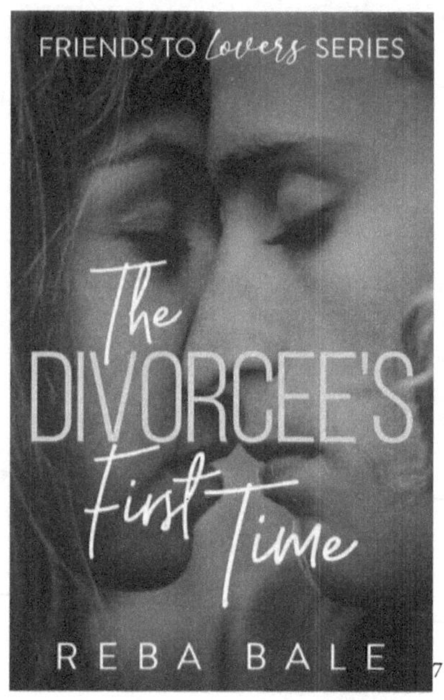

When Jennifer goes out with her best friend Susan to celebrate her divorce, she gets more than she bargained for. The dominant older woman gives Jennifer her first time lesbian experience and changes things forever. Will it be a one-time thing, or will their hot and steamy night lead to more? This friends to lovers novella is standalone romance intended for adult audiences only, due to explicit scenes and light BDSM.

---

6. https://books2read.com/u/bpznKX

7. https://books2read.com/u/bpznKX

Also by Reba Bale

Affair Recovery
Share Me: A Cheating Husband's Punishment

Dancing with Strangers
Taken by Surprise

Friends to Lovers
The Divorcee's First Time: A Hot Friends-to-Lovers Lesbian Romance
My BFF's Sister
My Rockstar Assistant
My College Crush
My Fake Girlfriend
My Secret Crush
My Holiday Love
My Valentine's Gift
My Spring Fling

Paying for Tuition

The Billionaire's Assistant
The Babysitter's Ride Home
The Babysitter's First Ménage
The Teaching Assistant's Lesson

Punishing Holidays
Turkey and a Spanking
Shopping and a Spanking

Sharing With Strangers
The Ride of My Life

Spanking Therapy Clinic
The Reluctant Bride's First Spanking
The Reluctant Bride Gets Caught
The Billionaire Gets Punished
The Curvy Reporter Gets Punished

The Divorce Recovery Team
Spanking Justice
A Punishing Workout
A Disciplined Budget

The Marriage Survival Retreat
Finding His Alpha

Watching His Wife
Exploring His Fantasy

The Voyeur Romance Series
Naughty Dinner Date
Naughty Laundry Day
Naughty Camping
Naughty Love Story
Naughty Sunbathing

Toys for Grown-Ups
Ménage a Geek
Financial Punishment

Unlikely Doms
Alpha in a Sweater Vest
Alpha Student
Alpha Yogi

Standalone
Hotel Spanking
Unlikely Doms
Divorce Recovery Team: A Punishment Experiment Collection
Spicing Up My Marriage
It Takes Three
The Christmas Swap

Sinful Desires